Wright on Time: ARI. ... om beginning
to end. Through travel and exploration of their world, the Wright
Family live a life of freedom on the road and are passionate about
learning in all that they do. I love how this book approaches
homeschooling as a common, valid option. The love, respect and
connection that the family shares is deeply touching as they support
one another throughout their expedition.

> - Dayna Martin, Author of *Radical Unschooling – A Revolution
>   Has Begun*
>   www.UnschoolingAmerica.com

At last! A beautifully written series of chapter books about
a homeschooling family traveling together. The respectful
communication and love in the Wright family while on a fun
mystery trip around the US will echo what young readers and
caring parents really know is true; Families can be fun! My 10 year
old loved it and is ready for the next one!

> - Rain Fordyce, Authentic Life Coach and Author of *I Am
>   Learning All the Time*
>   www.HomeschoolAdventureBooks.com

What a great joy it was to accompany the Wright family on their
first adventure in the caves of Arizona. I was both on the edge of my
seat at home ~deeply interested and often in suspense~ *and* right
there in Arizona with them, as they joyfully excavated their gems,
minerals and their own passions. With this delightful book, Lisa has
created a family that is interesting to the reader because they are
interested in the world. She has created a family that is a pleasure
to be around because they are respectful to one another and of

each other's individuality. I think that *Wright on Time: ARIZONA* is a beautiful example of how real learning is for everyone of every age...and how it can be found right there **in** the joyful living.

> - Anne Ohman, Mother of two always unschooled teenage boys, Founder/Owner of the *Shine with Unschooling* on-line community, Creator & Director of a respectful and celebratory parent/child library program, Inspirational Conference Speaker and Published Writer, currently completing two books-in-progress.
> www.ThisIsHowWeShine.com

What a great book to get the whole family excited about adventuring together. This engaging story has me looking forward to planning a spelunking trip of my own and sharing it with my family.

> - Barb Lundgren, Founder of the *Rethinking Education/ Rethinking Everything* yearly conference
> www.RethinkingEducation.net

Lisa M. Cottrell-Bentley

Wright on Time™

ARIZONA

Illustrated by Tanja Bauerle

ISBN: 0-9824829-0-6
ISBN-13: 9780982482902
Library of Congress Control Number: 2009928001

Visit www.WrightOnTimeBooks.com to order additional copies.

To my amazing daughter
Zoë
who inspired this book series and inspires me daily

ARIZONA

Arizona became a State on February 14th, 1912

Two-Tailed Swallowtail Butterfly State Insect

Saguaro Cactus Flower
State Flower

Petrified Wood
State Fossil

Ringtail
State Mammal

The Grand Canyon State

The Grand Canyon

Humphrey's Peak

Flagstaff

Mogollon Rim

Cactus Wren
State Bird

Phoenix
State Capital

Saguaro National
Monument

Turquoise
State Gemstone

Tucson

Kartchner's Caverns

Chapter One

The Wright family walked down the rock lined desert path toward the cave. Seven year old Aidan kept pulling ahead, anxious to be the first to see a bat.

Nadia hollered, "Wait up," and ran after him. Her little brother always wanted to be first everywhere they went.

Stephanie and Harrison, their parents, smiled as they held hands and followed behind. This was going to be an exciting adventure and today was just the first step. It was the first stop of their RV travels around the United States and they were excited to start the trip with a day of cave exploring in Arizona.

Stephanie looked at the surroundings and was in awe of the rugged beauty of the Arizona desert. People usually thought of deserts as nothing but sand dunes. However, the Sonoran was full of life. Cholla, ocotillo, prickly pear, and giant saguaros surrounded them. Out of the corner of her eye, a jack rabbit hopped away and a gecko scurried. Being late May, wildflowers covered the landscape and many cacti were in bloom. The warm breeze had a sweet scent making her feel very relaxed.

"There's one!" Aidan yelled.

Harrison let go of his wife's hand and ran ahead to his son. "I don't think it's a bat just yet," he said after catching up with Aidan. "It's too early in the day for bats. They usually only come out at night."

"What was it then?" Aidan asked.

"I don't know. Maybe it was a quail or a road runner?" Harrison responded. "It was really fast."

The cave's owner heard their conversation and joined the small group. "Hi, I'm Bob, you must be the Wright family."

"That's right, we're the Wrights," Nadia said with a grin. She could never resist the pun. "I'm Nadia, I'm

ARIZONA

eleven, and that's my brother Aidan, the bouncy one with the curly hair," she said as she pointed and flipped her long red hair over her shoulder.

Bob shook hands with the children and asked them about their goal in renting the cave for the day.

"I read that many caves in this area have gems and minerals. I'm hoping to find malachite and my brother wants to see…"

"Bats!" Aidan interrupted.

"Well you came to the perfect place. You will definitely find bats inside," Bob said. "This cave has been in my family for three generations. As you know, it is a fee dig site and we lease it out by the day, week, or month. I'll show you around a bit and then leave you alone to explore. Here is the gear you'll need."

Bob handed them each a helmet with a built-in miner's light and then held out a small pack which contained tools, gloves, and protective goggles. Harrison took the pack. Bob pointed to the screen trays and then the dozens of buckets, shovels, and small empty containers sitting near the entrance. "These are all at your disposal," he said.

"These are so freaky cool!" Aidan said as he put his hardhat on.

"Did you bring food and water?" Bob asked.

Wright 🐢 n Time

Stephanie held up her backpack. "We've got enough food for the whole day along with plenty of water. We even brought a squirt bottle of water."

"Oh, that's good. Squirting water on the cave surface can really help in finding gemstones."

"That's what I heard," Nadia said, now glad she had asked her mom to pack it.

Aidan turned on his headlight and dashed into the cave. Bob was happy to see people who were so excited about exploring his cave. Usually the only people who visited were prospectors looking to get rich and they didn't always have a natural appreciation for the beauty and wonder of cave life.

When Harrison had made the reservation, he'd sought out a cave which was safe and had no dangerous pits or crevices. He had been looking for a cave which was family friendly so he could write a magazine article about caving with children. This cave fit the bill perfectly. It had been well explored and mapped and would be perfect for the kids to wander around in. It was even salted, otherwise known as enriched, in certain marked areas of the cave. This meant that in addition to the native gems and minerals of the area, extra natural treasures had been planted for explorers to find. This would make the day's mining even more rewarding for them.

Bob handed Stephanie a laminated map of the cave and started pointing out significant locations. "As you probably know from our website, our cave has two 'great' rooms. The one you come to first is where most of the gems and minerals are found. The flags on the walls indicate the salted areas. You can mine wherever you want to, except where marked." He paused and then pointed again at the map, "The second big room is about two-tenths of a mile further and that is where the most bats live. There are several thousand in this cave community."

Aidan's ears popped up at that and he ran back to join his family. "Thousands?"

"Yes, thousands. It is also where most of the cave formations are located. Please be careful there and do not disturb or touch the stalagmites and stalactites," he paused. "Do you know the difference between the two?" he asked the children.

Nadia was the first to answer. "Stalactites are the ones on the ceiling growing down and stalagmites are on the floor growing up. Stalactites have a C for ceiling. Stalagmites have a G for ground. You might trip over a stalagmite, while bumping your head on a stalactite," she giggled and got out her notebook, ready to show Bob the notes she'd been taking in case he was interested.

Aidan ran back into the cave again. He wasn't interested in hearing about rock formations.

"Very good! That's exactly correct," Bob replied. "Did you learn that in school?"

"I don't go to school. My brother and I are homeschooled," Nadia said.

"That's great," Bob said. "Seems like more and more people are doing that these days."

"We're actually roadschoolers now that we are living in an RV," she corrected herself.

"That sounds fun!"

The group joined Aidan in the cave.

Only ten feet in and he'd already found something interesting. "What is this?" he asked to no one in particular. "It looks like gold!"

Bob answered. "Actually, it's iron pyrite, otherwise known as fool's gold. It's really common in this area and while beautiful, isn't worth much money. Go ahead and put some in your collection sack if you'd like." Bob continued, "Here let me show you a quick trick first." He reached down for a roll of toilet paper from a large box.

ARIZONA

"What are you going to do with that?" Aidan asked, intrigued.

"This is a miner's trick! If you find something particularly fragile, you can roll it in toilet paper to keep it safe. It makes a great padding for your treasure while you travel and it is easy and lightweight to carry. Here, go ahead and try it." He held out the roll to Aidan.

Aidan took the roll and wrapped his newly found piece of iron pyrite. He set his rock in a crate and went to find more, which were scattered all over the ground.

Harrison took the tools out of the bag and started looking at them. The kids joined in. Bob explained what each tool was for. He pointed at the combination rock pick hammers. "This will be your most useful tool today. It is a hammer on one side and a pick on the other. Hammer away at a large section of rock, then use the pick on the other side for digging out something specific."

He demonstrated on the iron pyrite, knocking off a large chunk. He handed the rock to Aidan.

"Freaky cool, another piece of iron pirate," Aidan said.

"Iron *pie-right*," Nadia corrected.

"I'm a pirate who wants some pie all right," Aidan said with a laugh. Bob and Nadia joined in.

Wright ❁n Time™

"In all seriousness," Bob said, "be sure to always wear your helmet and safety goggles whenever you are using these tools or are near someone who is using the tools. Those little chunks of rock can fly quickly! You'll want to wear your gloves then, too, or you'll get blisters."

They each put on a tool belt and put their rock hammer picks into their special belts.

Bob continued, pointing at the screens and buckets and canvas knapsacks. "Take the buckets and sacks for collecting your specimens in. Once you have a full bucket, you can bring it back to the cave entry. Over there," he pointed just outside the cave, "is the screening area. You can use the screens to sift and sluice out more gems and minerals. There is a hose with running water there. Do you know how to do that?"

Stephanie, an athletic and avid participant in lots of adventure sports, had done some mining years before and she shared her story with Bob.

"Well, that's about it then. Have fun! I keep the entry locked from looters when someone isn't inside. My wife or I will be locking it again around dusk, so please be out by then. We'll holler in since cell phones don't work inside the cave. The echoing nature of the cave makes it so you should all be able to hear each other at all times if

ARIZONA

you holler. Oh, yeah, and the bathroom is located on the north side of road, close to where you parked."

"Thanks! Bye," the Wright family said to Bob. They were anxious to get started exploring on their own.

Chapter Two

After they said goodbye to Bob, Aidan and his mom immediately started walking deeper into the cave. Stephanie's light had been off until then and the pure darkness of the cave was shocking. Without her headlamp, she couldn't see her own hands in front of her face. Aidan and Stephanie were completely out of the others' lights and the light from the cave entrance. They began playing around with their headlamps.

"I see spots when we turn both lamps off," Aidan noticed.

"Those are called afterimages," his mom said.

"Freaky weird. Let's do it again."

"Okay," she said.

"Freaky awesome!"

While they were playing with their lights, Harrison and Nadia spent more time looking at the iron pyrite. Nadia wanted some for her collection also. Even though she knew it wasn't real gold, she was amazed at how it looked when their lights shone on it just so.

"It's so sparkly and pretty," Nadia said to her dad.

"I wonder why it isn't worth much," Harrison replied to his daughter. "Do you think it is because it is so common?"

"Maybe," she said with a smile. She would have to find out more about iron pyrite. She always loved to uncover facts about new things.

It wasn't long before they all met up together again in the first great room. Harrison found the battery operated lamps in the room and turned them all on. The middle of the room was quickly illuminated, making long shadows in the corridors and against the walls. Aidan thought this was the best place to make shadow puppets on the walls.

"Look at my rabbit!" He showed his family.

ARIZONA

"Neat," replied Nadia. "I can make a butterfly." She made her hands flutter around the room like a butterfly as Aidan's bunny hopped. She stopped when she saw something glimmer.

Nadia took out her pick and goggles, and then started pounding on the cave wall.

"What have you found, Nadia?" Stephanie asked as she went over to investigate.

"I don't know yet," Nadia said as she continued pounding the wall.

Little bits of dust clouded around her and larger bits of rock fell to the floor. The air smelled different deep inside the cave. It was sort of musty and humid, unlike the dry desert they'd just stepped out of. It was also significantly cooler than outside. They were glad to have long pants and sweaters.

Stephanie joined in the picking. Soon they had a nice sized pile of rubble. Nadia and Stephanie squatted down and sifted through the dirt. Nadia reached in and held up a dark red gemstone which was the size of a large marble.

"I think it's a ruby!" Nadia declared.

"Let me see! Let me see!" Aidan said as he ran over to them jumping up and down.

"Maybe it's a garnet?" Stephanie asked as she looked the gem over.

"I can't believe you found something so valuable so quickly," Harrison said, joining them.

"Wow!" Aidan said.

"It's beautiful," they all agreed as they admired the stone, wondering what it was for sure.

"If I found this so easily," Nadia said, "I wonder if there are more?" She wanted to get digging again as soon as possible.

Within thirty minutes, Nadia and Stephanie had collected a small pile of tiny red stones. Some were translucent like a diamond and some were solid and nearly orange. Aidan had none and he was getting impatient.

"I'm tired of digging. I want to find some bats," he said to his dad. "Let's go to the other room."

It was decided that they would go on to find bats and Stephanie and Nadia would meet them in the large room in another half an hour.

Aidan skipped ahead deeper into the cave with only his headlight lighting the way. He noticed that it began to smell different. As he stopped to smell the air more, he heard a strange sound.

Chapter Three

Aidan and Harrison heard and felt the bats before they saw them. Little fluttery gusts of wind coming from all directions, combined with tiny peeps and squeaks, made them realize they were in a different world. The normally boisterous boy became completely silent.

Harrison reached out for his son's hand and pulled him closer as they quietly crept further and further into the second great room.

"Do you see?" the dad whispered almost inaudibly as he raised his headlamp and pointed to the ceiling. He pushed his glasses higher on his nose so he could see more clearly.

After a silent minute, Harrison took off his light and kept it pointed toward the ceiling as he turned and looked at Aidan. The boy's eyes were huge, his mouth was agape, and he looked unable to move.

"You okay?" Harrison asked quietly as he kneeled down so that their faces were closer together.

Aidan nodded.

"Sure?"

"Yes," Aidan barely voiced. Then he shook his head no and whispered, "This is freaky awesome! I can't believe it."

Thousands of bats hung on the super tall ceiling. Many were holding on to other bats and gathered in clumps of all sizes. A few darted back and forth. The two humans stood there in silence for a long time. They were concentrating on the bats so much, they didn't hear Nadia and Stephanie approaching them a while later.

"And to think you were worried we might not see any bats," Nadia said in a normal tone, which seemed unbearably loud as it broke the silence.

Aidan jumped. "Shhhhhhh!" he whispered. "We're listening to the bats."

ARIZONA

"Sorry," Nadia whispered back, "but, wow! This is sure amazing, isn't it?"

Nadia pointed to the side. When Aidan looked to where she pointed, he saw amazing rock formations.

"They must be thousands of years old. Some are nearly ten feet tall," Nadia said.

The four cautiously and quietly stepped further into the room, afraid of disturbing the bats' sleep. They stepped within a few feet of a waterfall of stalactite and stalagmite formations and examined them closely without touching them.

"These are the stale… egg… mites you've been talking about?" Aidan whispered to Nadia.

Nadia tried not to giggle. "Stal-AG-mites, not *stale egg mites*," she corrected him. "They are formed by the slow dripping water filled with minerals over a very long time."

Aidan finally understood what his sister had been talking about for the last month. "Oh, wow! They're much neater than any old egg mites," he said.

"I tried to explain it to you, but all you could think about was bats."

"Bats are cool," he simply said keeping his voice low. "I wonder if Batman lives in a cave like this?"

Wright ❀n Time

"I think Batman's cave is probably a little more decked out," Harrison replied with a smile.

"Probably with a bathroom and kitchen," Stephanie agreed.

"So long as it has bats like these," said Aidan as he stretched out his arms as if hugging the whole room. There were just so many of them. He wondered what it would be like to sleep underneath a ceiling of bats, listening to their flapping wings and feeling the soft gusts of breeze. He sighed with pleasure and closed his eyes to listen more closely.

A minute later, Aidan opened his eyes and stared at the bats again. He stared for a long time before he dropped his arms and began to explore the rest of the big room. The boy examined all the nooks and crannies and wondered if any bugs or snakes lived in the cave, too. He didn't see any, but he knew that didn't necessarily mean anything.

Stephanie decided to take a few photographs of the rock formations while Nadia took notes in her journal. The girl made a few sketches of the speleothems — a fancy word for cave formations — and wrote down her thoughts and estimations on the size of the cave's walls and decorations. She knew they had a map with detailed dimensions, but she enjoyed making her own estimates before checking out the answers.

"Hey, Dad," Aidan quietly said. His enthusiasm made him want to be loud, but the sleeping bats held him back. It was difficult for him to contain his excitement.

Harrison went over to his son.

"Are we allowed to dig in this room, too?" he asked.

"Yes, but only in this area here by the flag, not over by your sister and mom."

"Fantastic," he said, "because I see black onyx."

"Black onyx? Where?" Harrison asked. This potential discovery piqued his interest.

Aidan pointed out the find and the two started gently picking at the rock around the shiny black. They were very gentle, trying to be as quiet as possible so as to not disturb the bats.

As they hammered and picked at the crumbly rock, the black object took on shape. It was a lot larger than either of them expected.

"Is this an area that was planted with gems and minerals?" Aidan asked.

"Yes," replied Harrison.

"They're still real though, aren't they?"

"Oh, definitely, yes," his dad replied. "Anything found here is found in nature."

As they continued digging the black object out of the wall, Aidan was the first to notice that it probably wasn't a natural object. "Dad, I think there are words or something on this thing."

They stopped digging and Harrison directed a light on it. About a one inch square of the object could be seen. It was smooth and cool to the touch, just like a gem, but there was definitely some type of manmade marking on it.

"What is it?" Aidan asked.

Harrison had no idea and told his son that. How could something manmade get embedded in a rock? Perhaps the rock wasn't really rock, but rather compressed dirt. He had no clue as to what this was or how it got there.

They pondered what they should do.

"Should we leave it?" Aidan asked.

"I don't know," said Harrison. "Bob said we could have anything we found in the dig areas, so let's get it out of the wall and then we can decide what to do with it. Sound good?"

"Okay," said Aidan.

ARIZONA

The two kept picking, alternating their strokes while being careful and cautious not to damage their discovery. The thrill of finding something kept Aidan's interest and they lost track of the time.

"Find something interesting?" Nadia asked as she and her mom strolled up to them a while later.

"We've found a black thing, but we don't know what it is," said Aidan.

Right then, the object broke free from the wall and fell to the ground with a clunk.

Chapter Four

They all four shone their lights on the object. It wasn't completely black afterall. Only the front — or perhaps it was the back — was black. Aidan was the first to touch it. He was curious about this strange find and he flipped the object in his hands. The other side looked gold or maybe it was bronze or even copper. The whole thing was only about two inches square and a half of an inch thick.

"It looks like someone lost a cell phone or MP3 player or something," Aidan suggested.

"That would be a strange thing to find in here," said his dad.

"Is it heavy?" asked his mom.

Aidan weighed it in his hand. "No, it's light." He handed it over to his mom.

"It barely weighs anything," she remarked, handing it over to her husband.

"Check out the turtle," Aidan said, mentioning the drawing on the object.

Harrison examined the curious object as closely as he could without really proper lighting. His pointer finger stroked the object. "It feels completely smooth to the touch, and the symbol is also completely flat and it looks Mayan."

Nadia leaned in. She and her dad shared a love of linguistics and writing. They loved the puzzle of deciphering old languages and learning about the cultures who invented them. Her finger reached out to stroke the symbol, too. "Weird that it is completely flat. It does look slightly Mayan, but not quite," she continued to her dad. "Have you ever seen a little gadget like this before?" she asked her mother, the gadget expert in the family.

"No, I haven't," said Stephanie, quite perplexed. She was a telecommuting software engineer and was always

ARIZONA

up-to-date on the latest electronic gizmos and gadgets available, some often before they were on the market. If a new device existed, she was usually one of the first people to know all the details about it. In her job, she helped design software which went into small portable electronic devices, so she was familiar with many small computers and electronics of this size.

Stephanie took the square object back and attempted to turn it on. She couldn't find any obvious buttons or switches and no matter what she did, the device didn't respond. It appeared to be solid with no seams, yet its colors were different on different parts. It was baffling to them all.

"Well, let's see what Bob has to say about it," Harrison suggested.

They all agreed. Stephanie gently rolled the object in toilet paper, and then carefully set it in the camera pack next to her camera. She wanted to make sure that this didn't get broken, whatever it was.

Chapter Five

"**I**'m starving!" Aidan declared.

"So am I," said Nadia. "Where is the bag with the sandwiches?"

"It's back in the first great room," replied Stephanie. "Let's take our things and head back there. The water is in there, too."

The four were feeling quite comfortable in the cave by this point and the walls felt familiar and safe. Aidan skipped ahead of his family, determined to set up their picnic before they got there.

"What do you think that thing you found is?" Stephanie asked Harrison as they slowly followed Aidan. Since he was fluent in several languages and had an interest in linguistics, she thought he might know what the symbol meant.

Harrison was hoping Stephanie would know more about the device than him, since she was a computer expert. He was actually surprised when she didn't immediately know what it was and what it did. "I don't recognize the mark on it. I'll have to get a better look at it in the light," he said.

"Do you think someone accidentally left it behind?"

"I would have thought that, but it took Aidan and I a while to uncover it. It was really buried, like it had been there for a long time. It must be old, but it doesn't look old. It's odd."

"It is really weird. We'll definitely have to ask Bob about it," Stephanie agreed.

"I think it's an old radio," Nadia piped in as they strolled along in the cave.

"It was buried enough for me to think that, too," Harrison agreed, "but it is significantly smaller than any old radio I've ever seen."

"There's also no antenna on it," said Stephanie.

ARIZONA

"None we can see," said Nadia.

Just then, they heard a scream. The three went running toward the cave's main room.

"Aidan! Aidan! Where are you?" they each called out.

"Ahhhhhh!" they heard again. It was definitely Aidan screaming.

"Where are you?" Stephanie sounded frantic. She was scared something bad had happened and she became disoriented and wasn't immediately sure which way to run.

The echoing scream sounded like it was coming from all directions. They were certain that Aidan had been going toward the main great room, but they could hear his voice behind them as well.

"Aidan, stay calm. Where are you?" Harrison asked with a calm tone. He grabbed Stephanie's and Nadia's hands and put his finger on his lips to show them he wanted them to stay quiet. He always acted rational in stressful situations.

They heard Aidan again, coming from all directions.

Harrison asked again where he was.

"I'm in the big room," Aidan finally said, his voice sounded all shaky. "I think."

They picked up the pace and walked quickly toward the direction where they knew he was.

"You don't think a looter got in the cave, do you?" Stephanie whispered with worry in her voice.

Harrison shook his head no. "Are you okay?" Harrison asked Aidan, continuing to try and keep everyone calm.

The boy hesitated. He felt silly now. "Yes, I just got scared. My light went out and I tried looking for you and then something touched me."

"We're almost to you," Nadia called out.

"Ahhhhhhhhhhh!" Aidan screamed again. "It touched me again. And now something glowy is moving! Ahhhhhhhh!"

They let go of hands and ran toward Aidan as fast as they could. They quickly found the boy standing lightless near one of the cave's marking flags.

With the light of his family's headlamps, it was obvious what scary entity had been brushing into Aidan over and over. He'd been stepping into the flag's red fabric making it whoosh slightly against his face, scaring the boy silly.

Aidan started laughing as soon as he saw what had happened. Once he was happy, the rest felt happy, too, and they laughed with him.

ARIZONA

Harrison took Aidan's headlight and discovered the only problem with it was that the batteries had died. Taking new ones out of their bag, he replaced the batteries in Aidan's light. Stephanie turned the room's lights back on while Nadia kept Aidan busy creating shadow puppets again.

Stephanie laid out a thin blanket on the cave's floor and set out crunchy peanut butter and prickly pear jelly sandwiches for them all, with hot pepper sauce on the side for Harrison. No matter what the meal consisted of, Harrison would always eat it if he had hot pepper sauce to put on it. His family sometimes wondered if he didn't have as many taste buds as the rest of them since he always seemed to like his food hotter than anyone else.

Nadia snapped open four collapsible camping cups and filled them each with cold water. To complete the meal, Aidan put a small handful of carrots on the side of each person's sandwich. It was one of Stephanie Wright's classic meals: simple, easy, tasty, and nutritious.

The family sat in a circle on their blanket and hungrily ate every morsel of their picnic, while the two adults continued to scramble their brains for an idea of what it was that Aidan had found in the bats' room.

Chapter Six

Satiated from their meal, they each had different things they wanted to accomplish during their last hour in the cave.

Nadia really wanted to try and find malachite, her favorite mineral. Malachite's green coloring matched her eyes perfectly. When it was polished, it looked marbleized and calm like the depths of a sea. She loved how unique it was and how few people seemed to appreciate it.

Aidan wanted to see the bats again. Stephanie wanted to shoot some more photographs of the amazing cave formations. Harrison wanted to look around and see what they hadn't explored yet.

Aidan and Stephanie picked up the picnic and all the food packaging, making sure they'd left nothing behind.

"Who wants to go exploring?" Harrison asked.

"Me," the other three answered in unison.

It was decided the mother and son would go one direction and father and daughter another.

There was a small, almost unnoticeable, hole in one of the walls of the room they were currently in. Aidan found it and Stephanie, consulting her map for safety, said he could go into the hole. He fit easily into the hole, but Stephanie wasn't sure she would get through so well.

"Come on, Mom, you can do it," Aidan said urging her on.

Stephanie took off her pack, gently tossed it to Aidan through the hole, and then squeezed her thin body through.

They weren't expecting much, and were dazzled at the sight in front of their eyes. The crevice of the squeeze-through continued up nearly twenty feet to a cathedral ceiling with spires of soda straw formations hanging several feet down in length. The light from their head lamps made the water on the formations sparkle. The whole ceiling, which went on for what seemed like at least fifty feet, glittered like a chandelier.

"Wow," Stephanie said in awe.

"Freaky awesome!" Aidan replied.

"I had no idea this was here. It just says 'Whisper Corridor' on the map. It also says we aren't allowed to hunt for gems and minerals in this section. I can see why."

"Are those the stal-ag-mite things again?" Aidan asked. "They look a lot different than the other ones."

"They do start with S, but they aren't stalactites or stalagmites, at least not yet. They're called soda straws."

"Like soda pop straws?"

"Yes, exactly like drinking straws. That's where they got their name. They are even hollow like straws and extremely fragile. If they get plugged up, they'll turn into stalactites. Actually, I think they are sometimes called tubular stalactites."

"So, how are they made?" he asked.

"See the water that's dripping?"

The boy nodded. "Yes."

"There are minerals in that water. They slowly build up over time and create the formations. Sort of like that bathtub ring we were always trying to clean away at our old home in Tucson. But, we definitely don't want to touch these, since the oil from our hands would make them stop growing."

"So, could we stop cleaning and grow some soda straws in our shower in the RV?" Aidan asked. "We could always just use camping ground showers!"

Stephanie laughed. "Well, hmm... I don't think I want to wait a few hundred years before showering in our RV again to find out if we have enough minerals in our water to grow one."

"Can the straws grow on the floor, too?"

"No, they can't, but they sometimes fall onto the floor and the minerals in the dripping water also create the stalagmites."

"That's freaky cool!" Aidan said.

The ground was rocky and rough in this new room, not at all smoothed out like the rest of the cave. It was clear this little passage was untouched. The two crept along slowly. They couldn't keep their eyes off the ceiling.

After a few minutes, Aidan skipped ahead and tripped over a rock which was sticking out of the floor. Never seeming to feel pain and always the jokester, he laughed. "I think I might have found a stalag-might," he said.

His mother couldn't help but laugh. "Oh, Aidan."

ARIZONA

"It's just so," he paused, "well," he paused again walking forward some more and moving his hands in emphasis, "freaky awesome in here!"

"It certainly is," Stephanie agreed as she nodded.

They continued walking to the end of the corridor. The crack in the ceiling swept down at this point, hiding its way into the wall.

"You'd never know this was here if that hole in the wall wasn't there. Amazing!" Stephanie said. "It's just like a giant geode."

"I wonder how many other places like this exist that no one even knows about."

"Good question!"

Stephanie took out her camera and started taking some photographs.

"There aren't any bats in here," Aidan noticed. "I wonder why."

"I don't know. We'll have to ask Bob."

"Good idea!" he said.

Meanwhile, Nadia and Harrison hung out in the large great room, using their picks on various spots on the wall, trying to find malachite.

It had been several minutes and neither of them had found anything interesting. Nadia got the squirt bottle and sprayed some water on a little concave section of the wall. The water made everything a little shinier and she could tell the different colors apart from each other easier since the dust was washed away.

She was covering the wall with a thin veil of water when Harrison walked up to her.

"Look!" Nadia said with excitement. "There's something green here."

"Sure is," Harrison replied. He got out his pick to help Nadia uncover this new green find. It looked really fragile, so they had to be really careful.

"Freaky awesome in here," a whispered voice said.

The father and daughter looked at each other. Nadia's eyebrows went up and she pushed her long red hair behind her shoulder. They twirled around, expecting to see that Aidan had snuck up on them, but he wasn't there.

"That was strange!" Harrison exclaimed.

They shrugged their shoulders at each other and continued digging.

It took several long minutes, but soon they had picked a small circle around the green object.

ARIZONA

"I wonder if this is a gem or a mineral or something weird again," Nadia pondered.

"I'm thinking it might be a mineral, but I thought that black thing Aidan found was onyx. So, you never know," Harrison said.

"What do you think the black thing is?" Nadia asked as she continued picking around the stone in the wall.

"I don't know. With those markings, we might ask my friends, Dr. Arte and Dr. Maeve Smith. You remember Arte from the Museum of Archeology and Paleontology in New York, don't you? Maeve is his wife."

"I do remember him. We're going to see him in Utah next month, aren't we?" Nadia asked.

"Yes, we are. Maeve is a linguist from New York. She'll also be at the dinosaur dig by the time we get there. Let's show her it when we get there."

"Show who, what?" Stephanie's voice said, out of nowhere.

Nadia and her dad looked at each other again.

"Where did Mom's voice come from?" Nadia asked.

"Ooo-ooo-ooh, from over here," a voice whispered with a ghostly haunt.

Both Harrison's and Nadia's eyebrows were up now.

"All right, what's going on?" Harrison asked.

Chapter Seven

Laughter out of nowhere surrounded them. The laughing parties could hardly contain themselves. "It's the Whispering Corridor," Aidan blurted.

"Where are you?" Nadia asked with a quizzical look on her face.

"We went through the hole in the north wall. Apparently you two are at the sweet point in the great room on the south side. I can hear you perfectly from in here," Stephanie said.

"So can I," said Aidan.

"That is so cool," said Nadia.

"Freaky cool!" said Aidan.

"Indeed," the parents said simultaneously.

They all started laughing again.

When the Wright family was done playing with the acoustics in the Whisper Corridor, Aidan and Stephanie left the secret chamber and joined the other two in the great room. By the time they got to them, Nadia had extracted a small spiky green mineral.

"Check this out!" Nadia said as she held up the pale green thing with gloved fingers.

"What is it?" Aidan asked.

"It is green," answered Nadia.

"I know it's green, but what mineral is it?"

"I don't know. I'll have to look it up or maybe Bob will know."

Aidan told her all about the soda straws they discovered while Nadia carefully laid the mineral safely in a small container by itself. She was worried packing it, even in toilet paper, would break the spikes off since it looked so fragile. They decided to leave it in the great room while they explored more of the cave.

"What do you want to do now?" Harrison asked them.

ARIZONA

"I want to see the bats again!" Aidan replied.

"I want to see the soda straws and try to find malachite," said Nadia.

"I got some excellent photographs of the soda straws, so I'm happy," said Stephanie. "But, I'm willing to go back in there again, if you want."

"No, I'd like to see them. You go with Aidan to see the bats, okay?" Harrison asked.

"Sounds good. See you here in twenty minutes. That's all the time we have left."

They went their separate directions again.

Nadia and Harrison immediately headed for the Whispering Corridor. They wanted to check out the soda straws that Aidan couldn't stop talking about. Harrison, being tall, had to really squeeze in order to fit through the hole in the wall.

"Wow! This really is neat," Harrison said as he joined Nadia in the corridor.

"It sure is. I can see why Mom and Aidan spent so much time in here. It's amazing."

The two walked up and down the short path quickly and then squeezed their way back into the great room. Nadia went through the crack in the cave wall first. By the time her dad made it through, she was engrossed in something on the wall next to the flag that designated a salted area.

"What are you looking at there?" Harrison asked.

"I think I've discovered the solution to the mystery of the 'glowy thing' that Aidan saw earlier," Nadia said.

"Oh, what is it?"

"Scorpion!"

"A scorpion? Really?" he asked as he stepped closer.

"Yes. When I stepped out of there," she said as she pointed to the Whispering Corridor, "I saw a tiny glow that was moving. So, I came over closer to see what it was."

Harrison looked toward where Nadia pointed as he pushed his glasses up onto his nose again. Sure enough, it was a scorpion.

"I didn't think scorpions came this far into caves," Harrison said.

"And I didn't think they could glow without a black light," Nadia said.

"Anomaly," they replied at the same time. Sometimes Harrison and Nadia thought a lot alike!

They continued watching the lone scorpion climb into a small crevice in the wall until it was time to pack up.

ARIZONA

Aidan and Stephanie looked up at the bats as they entered the bats' room again.

"I didn't realize we were going to be spending so much time looking up today," Stephanie said. "I'm getting a crick in my neck." She rolled her head from side to side, making her short blonde hair bob back and forth.

"It makes me dizzy, but I love it." Aidan enjoyed spinning and twirling, especially while looking at the ceiling watching the bats.

After a few minutes, they sat on the ground, content to spend their last few minutes in the cave watching the mammalian wonders.

"Well," Stephanie said as she looked at her watch. "It looks like it's time to go."

"Aww, man!" Aidan was disappointed, but understood. He gathered his things to go.

They made their way back to the great room just as Nadia and Harrison were picking up the last of their supplies and finds. Together, they all started back toward the cave entrance. They were all quiet and contemplative. Even though they were tired, they'd enjoyed their time in the cave so much, they hated the idea of leaving.

Wright :n Time

"I'm disappointed I didn't find any malachite, but I sure had fun," said Nadia.

"You found that freaky weird spiky thing and I found that freakociously weird black thing," said Aidan.

"And don't forget the bats," said Harrison.

"And the Whispering Corridor," said Stephanie.

"Who could forget?" Aidan asked.

"Not me! I can't believe those soda straws, either. There are thousands and they are so long!" said Nadia.

Just then they felt a breeze and heard squeaky sounds. They were getting louder and closer.

Chapter Eight

The bats were waking up for the night. The commotion was fairly loud.

"Is everyone out?" they heard a woman's voice calling.

"We're still here," the Wrights called back as they hurried toward the entrance.

"Looks like they're out of the cave, then," the woman's voice said. "Must be out hiking on the mountain somewhere."

"No, we're in here! We are in here!" Harrison called.

The echo of clinking keys was very clear. The family looked at each other, wondering what to do. They dropped their things and they all started running toward the entry, calling out, "We're still in here! We are still in here!"

Bats swooped around their heads, making the areas with low ceilings difficult to navigate. The sudden squeaks from the bats made the key jingling sound nonexistent. Had the woman locked them in? Aidan wondered how the bats were going to get out if the people were getting locked in.

They didn't know the woman's name, so Nadia made one up, "Bob's Wife! We're still in the cave!" she called.

Stephanie was able to make it to the entry first since she ran for exercise every day. Her family was close behind. She saw the gate was closed and the padlock was locked. She squinted as the blinding sun blocked her view. She continued to cry for Bob's wife, but the woman didn't seem to hear her.

All four called out for what seemed like forever. When it was clear the woman was gone they sat, dejected, near the entry of the cave.

"I think we're locked in for the night," Stephanie said. She immediately wished she had brought more than just sweaters and a thin picnic blanket for her family. While it was still relatively warm at the moment, she knew the desert wouldn't hold its heat at night and it would soon be quite cold outside. Suddenly the sweaters they were wearing seemed very thin indeed and she gave an involuntary shudder.

Harrison put his arm around his wife. "It'll be fine. We are all together. When we're together, nothing bad can happen." He smiled at her.

"You're right, of course." She smiled back, but she couldn't hold back a subtle shiver.

"At least the bats are fine," said Aidan as he pointed up. "See how they are flying through the top of the gating. It looks like it was made special for them."

"They fly through the entry like there is nothing there," Nadia said.

"Look at them go," said Harrison.

"So, are we spending the night in the cave?" Aidan asked with wonder in his voice. He was excited by the prospect and his wide mouthed grin showed it. His face and hands were covered in dirt, yet his brown curly hair never looked mussed up.

"Looks that way," said Nadia trying to sound mature. She wasn't too keen on the idea of sleeping on a cold floor with bats flying over her head all night, but she was determined not to show it. "Where do you think we'd be the most comfortable?" she asked her parents.

"I'm not sure. Maybe in the first great room," said Harrison.

Harrison and Nadia started back toward the room to check out their options and to regather their supplies. When they were almost out of sight, Stephanie's voice called them back. "I see someone outside of the cave, come back! Come back!"

Chapter Nine

"**W**e're here! We're in the cave!" Stephanie called to the person outside the cave. Aidan jumped up and down and waved his arms, hoping it would draw the person's eyes toward him.

Slowly, an older lady made her way to the cave. Stephanie stopped calling out for her once it was obvious she was heading in their direction. Nadia and Harrison were back at the gate to see the good news.

"I'll run back and get our things from the cave while you talk with Bob's wife," Stephanie said. She then went back into the cave and collected the rest of their possessions and findings they had dropped in haste.

Bob's wife started talking when she was about twenty feet away from the cave's entrance. "Good thing you didn't turn off that light, young man, or I never would have known you were there," she said to Aidan. "I looked around the path, but didn't see any signs of you all, so I figured you were hiking on the mountain. You've done a great job of respecting the land. I didn't know you were still here."

"We're so glad you saw us!" Nadia said with relief in her voice.

"What's that, honey?" Bob's wife asked.

"We're so glad you saw us!" Nadia repeated a little louder.

"Oh, I don't know why I bother to ask questions when I'm so far away," she said to herself. "I can't hear a thing these days unless I'm right next to the person talking." She muttered a few more sentences to herself, but they couldn't tell what she was saying.

"It's so nice to meet you. We're the Wrights," Stephanie said as loudly as she could without screaming once the woman was closer.

ARIZONA

"Oh, I'm just tickled to be meeting you, too, honey! Can you imagine if I hadn't noticed that young man there with his headlamp? Since I'm here now, let me know, did you find anything interesting in the cave?" Her Texan drawl was showing through her words.

She unlocked the padlock and reopened the cave's gate. The Wrights stepped out of the cave's entrance and joined the woman. They all had wide grins of relief on their faces.

Nadia decided to ask a question which had been on her mind. "We were wondering, is this a ruby?"

"Could you shine your light on it, honey?"

Nadia did.

"That looks like a ruby all right, but it's actually a garnet," Bob's wife answered. "Garnet gets mistaken for ruby a lot."

"How about this one?" Nadia asked as she handed her one of the solid reddish-orange stones she had found along side the translucent red stones.

"Oh, that's red jasper," Bob's wife said.

"Nadia's got a piece of jasper stored away, but it's black and white. How come they're different colors?" Aidan asked.

"There are lots of different kinds of jasper, it can be confusing," Bob's wife answered him. "Yours at home must be Dalmatian jasper. This one is a different kind of jasper."

"We should look up what makes them different colors," said Nadia, wondering if there were any libraries or Wi-Fi internet access points nearby where she could read more about it.

"Show her the green one," Aidan said.

Nadia held out the green stone she and Harrison had found. "I know this isn't malachite. When I first saw it, all I saw was green. I was really hoping to find malachite. Malachite is, by far, my favorite mineral. It is the most beautiful and interesting one, because of its swirls of green. It's like marbleized marble. But, anyway..." She finally stopped and took a deep breath. She noticed she was getting long winded, as she often did.

From the look of the smile on Bob's wife face, it seemed like she didn't mind the rambling. So, Nadia carefully held the stone closer to Bob's wife's face.

"Here it is and I'm not sure what it actually is. Do you know?"

"Ah! Honey, you found my favorite!" Bob's wife smiled wider. "It's wulfenite."

ARIZONA

"Like a dog? *Woof, woof, woof,*" Aidan barked as he got down on all fours and ran around like a dog. His curly brown hair bounced as he trotted. The gaps where he'd recently lost his two bottom front teeth and one of his top front teeth could be seen when he barked loudly. "I'm a Dalmatian named Jasper! *Woof, woof.* And, Nadia, you're my friend *Woof-at-Night.*"

This made Bob's wife smile. "No, not like a dog. Not like a wolf, either," she was quick to add.

"I think I've read of it," Nadia said. "Isn't wulfenite a lead based mineral?"

"It is." Bob's wife was impressed. "Wulfenite is not a common mineral to find. Arizona is one of the few places in the entire world where it can be found."

"I had no idea it would be so spiky," Nadia said.

"Yes, spiky and fragile. You'll have to put it somewhere very safe. Be sure to keep it upright unless it's packed well. You are very lucky to have found green wulfenite. It's really rare. It's more commonly orange or yellow or brown. Here, come with me, honey."

She started rummaging around in a locked trunk just outside the cave. Nadia was intrigued by all the interesting containers the trunk held. There were so many different sizes and shapes. Stephanie stayed with Nadia while

Harrison went after Aidan, who was still pretending to be a dog.

"Hmm... Where is the one I need?" Bob's wife was talking to herself again. "Ah, here!"

"What is it?" Nadia asked.

"This is a special specimen container. The specialized foam in here will keep your mineral safe until you get it in a proper display case."

Bob's wife handed over the little clear plastic box to Nadia. The whole container was full of foam. Nadia was confused how this would keep the mineral safe. It looked like it would squish it, not protect it. "How does it work?" she asked.

"Oh, silly me!" Bob's wife opened the container and pointed at the foam. "You see, this isn't regular foam, this is special foam. As you set the mineral into it, it gives out and molds itself to the mineral's form. Here, let me show you."

Nadia handed over the wulfenite specimen.

Bob's wife gently set the mineral onto the foam in the box and softly pressed on a solid part. The foam looked like it melted under the mineral. Once the mineral was completely inside the case, she closed the clear lid. "Voila!"

ARIZONA

"Wow, that is really amazing!" Nadia said.

"It sure is," said Stephanie. "I've seen foam like this before in medical applications, but I had no idea it could be used for something like this, too."

Bob's wife beamed. She enjoyed wowing her customers.

"Thank you very much," Nadia said to her.

"No problem, honey. Oh, follow me!" She toddled off quickly.

"Where are we going?" Nadia tried to ask, but Bob's wife didn't hear her.

"Guess it's a surprise," Stephanie said to Nadia.

Nadia liked surprises.

Chapter Ten

Nadia and Stephanie followed Bob's wife back into the cave. She stopped right where Aidan, the dog, had gone off to bark. Harrison was smiling as he watched the boy. They were about ten feet into the cave.

"Sorry, guess we're in the way," Harrison said as he moved to get out of her way.

"No, no, honey, you're fine. What I want is right here." She smiled and pointed at the wall.

Nadia pointed her light at the spot where Bob's wife was pointing. The wall had green chunks everywhere.

Wright :n Time

"Malachite!" Nadia squealed with joy.

"Yes, now get to work, honey. So you know, this is a salted area of the mine. There are polished and unpolished specimens in this wall. All come from one of our other caves, right here in Arizona." Bob's wife beamed as Nadia and her mother started to dig out a particular malachite specimen Nadia wanted. "There are some beautiful blue azurite specimens there, too, since malachite and azurite are often found together."

Aidan took that opportunity to grab the woman's arm. "Bob's wife, I want to ask you something," he said.

She squatted down and looked Aidan in the eye. "Are you a little boy again, or are you still a little dog?"

"Boy. *Woof*! Just kidding, I'm both! But I'm a big dog, not a little one!" He panted a bit and woofed again for good measure.

The woman smiled. She enjoyed spending time with exuberant children.

"Aidan, we should really ask the nice lady what her name is. I don't think it's actually 'Bob's wife'," Harrison said.

"Oh, that's okay, honey," she patted Harrison's arm. "I get called that all the time. I don't mind." She smiled at them both and then turned to Aidan, "What did you want to ask me?"

"I was wondering," he paused, "why don't the bats live in the Whispering Corridor?"

"Oh, you found the secret corridor. Not everyone does, you know," she nodded knowingly. "You're a very curious boy, aren't you?"

Aidan nodded.

"Well, bats don't live in the Whispering Corridor because we've only just discovered the corridor a few months ago. Some Girl Scouts were exploring the cave and when one of them went to get a gem out of the wall, her pick went all the way through. She discovered the new part of the cave. Until then, there wasn't a way for people or bats to get into that area."

"Freaky cool! My sister is a Girl Scout." He thought for a moment. "Won't the soda straws get hurt if the bats go in there now?" Aidan wondered.

"Yes, they would, honey. However, we have a stable group of migratory bats who have lived in that particular part of the cave for as long as we know. We're fairly certain that they won't be interested in the corridor since they've already established a home in the second great room. Plus, no insects live in the corridor."

"Bats eat bugs, right?" he asked.

"Yes, they are insectivores."

"Oh Dad, ask Bob's wife about the black thing," Aidan said as he pulled on his father's arm.

"Yes!" Harrison said and he went to get the mysterious item from Stephanie's pack. He took it out and handed it over to Bob's wife. "Aidan and I found this embedded in the cave wall in the bat's room. Can we keep it?"

"As your contract says, anything you find during your time period, you can keep. We know there might be some great finds, but that makes life interesting doesn't it, honey?"

She looked over the item and wrinkled her gray eyebrows.

"Looks like a broken calculator or something."

"Or maybe a radio!" said Aidan.

"Either way, honey, it's yours." She handed it back to Harrison.

Harrison was hoping Bob's wife would be able to give information about the strange object, but was excited at the prospect of keeping it. He pushed his glasses up and stroked his black hair off his face. His eyes brightened at the thought of having a new mystery to solve.

ARIZONA

"Nadia," Harrison went over to his daughter, "we get to keep the device!"

"Oh, that's great!" Nadia joined in his excitement, "I can't wait to figure out what it is." She hugged him tightly.

Harrison held up the device in the faint light of the setting sun to try to get a better look at it. As he started to examine it, he heard Stephanie's pick. He turned to watch and put the device into his shirt pocket just as a new symbol started to glow dimly on its surface.

Stephanie hit her pick into the wall one more time and, with a plop, the malachite fell to the ground. She leaned over, picked up the mineral, and showed it to her daughter. Nadia let go of her dad and ran back to hug her mom. Her mother's chin rested on the top of her head perfectly.

"Oh, this is just the most perfect day!" Nadia jumped up and down and ran over to Aidan. "Look, look!" She held out the stone to show her brother.

"It's freaky cool!"

"Yes, it is! It's the best!"

They sat and inspected their gemstones while the adults picked up the remaining mining supplies.

The Wright family said goodbye to Bob's wife and walked away exhilarated, dirty and hungry.

"Let's go home," Stephanie said.

Stephanie's family smiled back at her. They'd been thinking the same thing.

Chapter Eleven

With their backpacks full of their cave findings, they grabbed each other's hands in happiness and walked in a tight row down the rock lined path back to the parking lot.

There in the parking lot their brand new home was waiting. A recreational vehicle they had only owned for a week was waiting for the Wrights to hop in and go on their next adventure. The copper colored vehicle stood proudly, gleaming like a flame gold streak in the Arizona setting sun. The little silver car the RV was towing reflected the pink of the sky like a mirror.

"I still can't believe that is going to be our home for the next few years," Stephanie said to her family.

"I know," Harrison agreed.

"I miss Connor already," Aidan said, thinking of his best friend in Tucson.

"We'll have to e-mail him tonight and tell him all about the bats and the cave," Nadia said. "I can't wait to e-mail Grandpa and Grandma and Kestrel and tell them about the jasper, wulfenite and malachite I found."

"Maybe you can send them some," Harrison suggested.

"Good idea, Dad."

Harrison unlocked the side door, and they each stepped in, taking off their shoes just like they did in their old non-drivable home.

"Prince Pumpkin the Third," Aidan called out to their pet turtle. "We're home! You'll never believe the things we saw!" He took the turtle out of his strapped down plastic container and started rubbing his neck.

Nadia got a piece of romaine lettuce and some peas out of the refrigerator for the turtle and fed him. Prince Pumpkin III chewed contemplatively, seeming to be

ARIZONA

listening to every word the children were telling him about their adventure. He was the smartest turtle they'd ever met, and it didn't surprise them one bit, considering he was over fifty years old.

"And Dad and Aidan found a weird MP3 player or phone or something with a picture of a turtle on it, and Mom and I found garnets and jasper, and we got locked in the cave and were worried we'd have to spend the night, and we were going to sluice, but never did, but that's okay because we had fun anyway, it was such a fun time, you would have loved it, well maybe not." Nadia gasped for breath. She'd strung their whole day into one rambling run-on sentence, telling the little turtle everything.

Even though they were tired, they took turns rinsing in their shower and putting on clean dry clothes. Cave exploring had proved to be one of the dirtiest activities they'd ever done. Aidan couldn't wait to do it again.

All clean, Harrison sat behind the driver's wheel. He punched the coordinates for Benson, Arizona, into the global positioning system and started up the RV. They'd be spending a night there on their way toward a dinosaur dig in Utah. Arizona was a big state, with a lot to see, so they were taking their time getting there.

"All buckled in back there?" he asked.

"We're ready!" the three in the back called to him. Off they drove to their next great adventure.

THE END

WRIGHT ON TIME BOOK 1: ARIZONA

GLOSSARY

acoustics [*uh*-**koo**-stiks]; the quality of sound in a room.

afterimage [**af**-ter-im-ij]; visual image seen after the original image is gone.

anomaly [*uh*-**nom**-*uh*-lee]; something different than what usually happens.

archeology [ahr-kee-**ol**-*uh*-jee]; careful study of past human life and cultures by examining found evidence.

azurite [**az**-*ur*-ihyt]; bright blue copper based mineral often found with wulfenite.

boisterous [**boy**-stir-*uhs*]; acting loud and joyful, sometimes rough.

cathedral (ceiling) [k*uh*-**thee**-dr*uh*l]; a really high ceiling, like in a church.

cholla [**choy**-yah]; spiny desert cactus.

concave [**kon**-keyv]; curving inward like the inside of a bowl.

corridor [**kor**-i-dor]; passage that connects several parts or rooms of a building.

ARIZONA

embedded [em-**bed**-ed]; inserted into an important part of the whole of something else.

freaky awesome, freaky cool, freaky weird, freakociously; fun phrases Aidan Wright uses. *Aidan saw a really neat object. "Freaky cool!" he said.*

gecko [**gek**-oh]; a small lizard.

insectivore [in-**sek**-t*uh*-vohr]; plant or animal that eats insects.

iron pyrite [**ahy**-ern] [**pahy**-rihyt]; Fool's gold; mineral that looks a lot like gold, but isn't. *Shouldn't be confused with metal pirates.*

jasper [**jas**-per]; crystal kind of quartz, usually red but can be many different colors, including black and white Dalmatian jasper.

laminate [**lam**-*uh*-neyt]; several layers of materials that are bonded together.

linguistics [ling-**gwis**-tiks]; the science of languages.

malachite [**mal**-*uh*-kihyt]; ore of copper, usually green.

mammalian [m*uh*-**mey**-lee-*uh*n]; having to do with mammals.

marbleized [**mahr**-b*uh*-liyzd]; patterned with streaks of colors in a special way.

Mayan [**mayh**-*uh*n]; having to do with the Maya people or their languages, located in Mexico and Central America.

migratory [**mahy**-gr*uh*-tohr-ee]; when an animal moves from one place to another, due to seasons.

MP3 player; device that plays audio files.

ocotillo [aw-k*uh*-**tee**-yoh]; spiny, woody plant that lives in the desert.

onyx [**on**-iks]; mineral, type of quartz. *The Wrights thought they had found pure jet black onyx.*

paleontology [pey-lee-*uh*n-**tol**-*uh*-jee]; study of life existing in former geological periods, using fossils.

ARIZONA

prickly pear [**prik**-lee] [pair]; cactus which has flattened and usually spiny stem joints. Usually green or purple. Jelly can be made from its fruit.

recreational vehicle (RV); large vehicle that people can travel and live in. *The Wright family lives in an RV.*

ruby [**roo**-bee]; red gemstone.

saguaro [suh-**wahr**-oh]; very tall cactus, often with arms.

salted cave; special cave that has had minerals, fossils, or other interesting objects planted for people to find.

satiated [**sey**-shee-*ey*-tid]; full and satisfied of food.

scorpion [**skor**-pee-*uh*n]; desert arachnid with a venomous sting.

soda straw [**soh**-d*uh*] [straw]; particular type of stalactite, hollow in the middle like a drinking straw.

Wright ☸n Time™

Sonoran desert [suh-**nohr**-uhn] [**dez**-ert]; desert in the southwestern United States and northern Mexico. *Not to be confused with yummy desserts, although eating a dessert in the desert is great fun.*

speleothem [**spee**-lee-o-thehm]; cave formation.

specimen [**spes**-uh-muhn]; a sample of an object that is studied and examined.

stalactite [stuh-**lak**-tihyt]; mineral deposit, often shaped like an icicle, hanging from the roof of a cave.

stalagmite [stuh-**lag**-mihyt]; mineral deposit formed on the floor of a cave from water drippings.

telecommute [**tel**-uh-kuh-myoot]; to work at home or on the road using a computer that is connected to a company's network.

tubular (stalactites) [**too**-byuh-ler]; tube shaped; see **soda straw** and **stalactite**.

ARIZONA

wulfenite [**wool**-*fuh*-nihyt]; lead based mineral, varies in color from gray to bright yellow, sometimes red, often spiky. *Nadia found a rare green specimen.*

What is that image the Wright family saw on the *mysterious* device?

In Arizona, the Wright family finds a *mysterious* device which shows an image of a turtle with a special symbol in the middle. The symbol is based off of an ancient Mayan glyph called a **Hunab Ku** symbol. The Mayans believed that the symbol represented the gateway to other galaxies beyond our own sun. Only the maker of the device understands why the Hunab Ku was drawn inside of a turtle. Check out **www.WrightOnTimeBooks.com** and read *Wright on Time: UTAH, Book 2* to find out more!

Join Nadia and Aidan as they continue their adventures in *Wright on Time: UTAH, Book 2* coming out Fall 2009. The Wrights have joined a dinosaur dig searching for allosaurus bones. Will they find any and what will they learn about that mysterious device? Be sure to check out **www.WrightOnTimeBooks.com** for even more fun, games, and a forum for you to post your own adventure tips!

MORE FACTS ABOUT ARIZONA

- Highest Point: Humphrey's Peak, 12,637 feet above sea level

- Lowest Point: Colorado River (near Yuma), 70 feet above sea level

- Size: 113,634.57 square miles (6th largest state)

- Residents are called: Arizonans

- 48th state to officially become a state

- Average Rainfall: 12.7 inches per year

- Longest River: Colorado River, 1450 miles

- Bordering States: California, Colorado, Nevada, New Mexico, Utah

- Bordering Country: Mexico

- State Amphibian: Arizona Tree Frog

- State Colors: Federal Blue and Old Gold

- State Fish: Apache Trout

- State Mineral: Copper

- State Neckware: Bola Tie

- State Tree: Palo Verde

Hey, Kids & Parents!

Have you been on any fun trips lately? Do you have a dream vacation? Going on a trip soon and looking for fun things to do?

Where do you think the Wright family should visit next on their RV trip around the USA? Is there a really fun place they should go to in your state?

Join the Forums on **www.WrightOnTimeBooks.com** and tell us all about your trips and all the fun places you've been! If you are younger than 13, be sure to get your parent's permission first.

Thanks!
Lisa

Dear Readers,

I hope you've enjoyed this book about my family. I've started my very own blog, telling all about places we've been and things we've seen that aren't in these books. I can't tell you where we are right now since that's top secret, but there are sure to be places that we've been that you'll find interesting.

To read more, and to tell me of places my family and I should check out (I love comments), see my blog at **www.WrightOnTimeBooks. com/nadia**. Aidan says he thinks it's freaky cool!

Love,
Nadia

CONTEST

Like this book? Want to see your name in print? The first child (13 and younger) from each state who reviews this book will have their review listed in *Wright on Time: UTAH, Book 2*. To be considered, please post your review on the **www.WrightOnTimeBooks.com** website as a blog comment in the Reviews section, or e-mail Lisa directly at **reviews@WrightOnTimeBooks.com**. Don't forget to add your review to the amazon.com page, too! You'll need to include your first name, your state, your age, and your review (no more than 3 sentences if possible).

The person who submits the 100th review (no matter where you live) will receive a free copy of *Wright on Time: UTAH, Book 2*. Lisa will contact you directly to get your details.

Please send Lisa your comments and questions at any time. She loves reading e-mails and seeing drawings from real kids just like you. She looks forward to hearing your thoughts and ideas!

TANJA BAUERLE is an active member of the Arizona chapter of the Society of Children's Book Writers and Illustrators and helps as Co-Illustrator Representative. After having lived in Germany and Australia, Tanja now calls Arizona home with her husband Kevin, her daughters Isabelle and Zoe, her two Goldens Otto and Peanut, and cat Ducky.

Tanja has had her own illustration and design business since 2003. Her love of story telling drives her to continually refine her craft. Her favorite mediums are acrylics, water color, and pen and ink, yet she loves digital tools also.

Check out **www.TanjaBauerle.com** for more information and to see some of her award winning work.

Photograph by Zoë Bentley, ©2009

LISA M. COTTRELL-BENTLEY has been writing since she was a child, winning her first writing contest at age 9. She's been writing professionally since 2002. Lisa is an active member of RWA and SCBWI.

Lisa and her daughters spent many hours searching for children's books about homeschoolers, but found very few. So, they decided to create their own. As they discussed their dream storylines, the *Wright on Time* series took shape. While they haven't found any mysterious devices *yet*, they have done lots of field research trying out many of the activities described in these books.

Lisa lives and learns while writing in southern Arizona with her husband Greg, two happy always homeschooled daughters Zoë and Teagan, and three cats. Her desire is for all people to live their own personal dreams, now and for always.

Looking for more right now? Check out
www.WrightOnTimeBooks.com!

NOTES